A Giant First-Start Reader

This easy reader contains only 35 different words, repeated often to help the young reader develop word recognition and interest in reading.

Basic word list for *Champ on Ice*

and	hoop	skate
backward	ice	skates
can	it	so
champ	jump	spin
dance	jumps	the
do	leg	there
faster	many	things
forward	none	through
go	on	twirl
goes	one	two
he	or	watch
him		with

Champ on Ice

Written by Sharon Peters

Illustrated by Diane Paterson

Troll Associates

Library of Congress Cataloging in Publication Data

Peters, Sharon.
    Champ on ice.

    Summary: Champ demonstrates his ice-skating skills.
    [1. Ice skating—Fiction.   2. Bears—Fiction]
I. Paterson, Diane, 1946-   ill. II. Title.
PZ7.P44183Ch   1988   [E]   87-10908
ISBN 0-8167-1093-7 (lib. bdg.)
ISBN 0-8167-1094-5 (pbk.)

There goes Champ.

Watch Champ go!

Champ can skate on ice.

He can do so many things on ice.

He can skate forward.

He can skate backward.

Champ can jump on ice.

Watch him jump through the hoop.

He skates faster and faster.

He jumps forward.

Can he do it? Watch!

There he goes through the hoop.

Champ can do many things on ice.

He can skate on one leg.

He can skate on two.

Champ can dance on ice.

He can dance with the hoop.

He can dance forward.

Watch him dance backward.

Champ can twirl on ice.

He can spin on ice.

Watch him spin and twirl!

He can spin and twirl on two legs . . .

or on one . . .

or on none!

There goes Champ.

Watch Champ go.

He can do so many things on ice!